Contents

I0623482

FRAGMENTS

Bataille believed that the true function of wealth was to "squander without reciprocation." Reading *Waste Extractions* I suspect that Andrea Mason agrees. Explicitly weird and wild, implicitly political, it is a work both formed and informed by an excessive cultural surplus and then re-collaged together by an undeniably British, art school educated brain. Exquisite re-giftings of DeLillo, Antonioni, and Cage, sit side by side with descriptions such as "Dirty. Pubes." The word 'cough' appears 37 times. A rotting seal carcass is vividly depicted… In short, I loved this book and hope you will too.

— Susan Finlay, *The Jacques Lacan Foundation*

Andrea Mason puts the flippin' 'eck into ekphrasis in these diverse, extraordinary responses to key works of film, music and literature.

— Nicholas Royle, *London Gothic*

A waste book in the tradition of Georg Christoph Lichtenberg's *Waste Books*—fragmentary, various, hybrid—taking additional power from waste as an urgent question: what is a waste of resources? of money? of time? A question that Mason answers in a glorious series of offcuts, scourings and scraps.

— Joanna Walsh, *Girl Online: A User Manual*

Andrea Mason's *Waste Extractions* is a brilliant and virtuoso performance drawn from her extraordinary repertoire of innovative approaches to fiction-making. Her pamphlet aptly concludes 'at the end: rapturous applause'. This refers perhaps to the John Cage piece rendered here through Mason's visually and sonically lively 'transcription', but 'rapturous applause' also seems a fitting response to the heightened, multisensory reading experience this pamphlet offers. *Waste Extractions* is not only a vibrant and engaging standalone piece, it also gives us an exciting glimpse into some of Mason's working practices, 'extracted' from her eagerly-awaited forthcoming hybrid-text /novel. She offers the reader a rich variety of methodologies as we are invited to consider if waste is simply the inevitable by-product of the 'decaying self': a necessary redundancy created by Gertrude Stein-like patterns of 'repetition with variation' characteristic of personal, linguistic and cultural processes. Or, whether it is the toxic consequence of the excess and damage caused by our environmental exploitation. Mason's pamphlet is by turn reflective and lyrical, playful and violent, making full use of the spatial potential of the page to challenge the 'wasteful' neglect of visual possibility in more conventional fiction. Like the best movie trailers, this pamphlet is both an adrenalin-packed world complete in itself, and a compelling hook for the bigger piece to come.

— Susie Campbell, *Enclosures*

ISBN: 978-1-915079-32-9

Cover design by Aaron Kent

Typeset by Aaron Kent

Edited by Cathleen Allyn Conway

brokensleepbooks.com

Broken Sleep Books
Rhydwen
Talgarreg
Ceredigion
SA44 4HB

Broken Sleep Books
Fairview
St Georges Road
Cornwall
PL26 7YH

Waste Extractions

Andrea Mason

Listen to the sound
of the earth turning

1963 spring

— Yoko Ono

FRAGMENTS

FRAGMENTS

What if a woman had to save the world? What if this woman, The Saver, went to her local waste facility, and said, *these workers are human too?* What if another woman, The Finder, wants to find The Saver, but The Saver eludes her? The Finder trawls through The Saver's archive, and makes attempts to meet, but the meetings are always cancelled. What is The Saver trying to teach The Finder? At The Finder's local waste facility, they conduct tours for avid schoolkids. The kids want to make even more waste to feed the machines.

~~Don de Lillo makes statements.~~

Brushing skin flakes off the bedsheet and pillow. Whose? Hers? An absent person's? A squeezing of the bum cheeks. Retention. Stand up. The cat wanders in, ruffled and dusty. The skin flakes are not the cat's.

If we organise our waste we will be organised. Waste is the key to unlock society's ills, and assess its functionality. In *Tales of the City*, Mona assesses Mary Ann's waste and creates a portrait of the lady. Our waste profiles us. We can be subjected to a waste analysis, from which a prescription can be issued: eat less processed food, read less crap magazines; lots of vegetable peelings, good, poo is no doubt regular.

I look at *Ada* by Atak based on *Ada* by Gertrude Stein. Now I listen to Gertrude Stein read 'Matisse'. I am a cultural accumulation. I can be that. And you can be certain that you can be certain. On the cover of Akutagawa's *Rashomon and 17 Other Stories*, a toothless hag: grey hair straggles either side of the mouth and furrowed brow; wide-open eyes are circles with black pin pricks at centre. On cue, a crow. *Caw caw caw.* I return to *Ada*. And *Tales of the City*: fizzy-poppy-gossipy.

In 'Rashomon', the woman sits with fire on a stick. Visceral details: a pus-filled pimple. Animal analogies: he moved "with all the stealth of a lizard"; "crouched, cat-like"; a "scrawny old woman" is "white-haired and monkey-like".

Bloody nature, swollen rivers, oozing mud, gorges, adrenaline, internality, going deep inside, waste, detritus, oozing pus. The pus-filled pimple, swelling, fit to burst, to splatter, to splay its yellow pus... onto what? Onto whom? Where?

Alexander Chee writes about his time as a student of Annie Dillard in an article. Chee informs us that she would count the verbs in their manuscripts. *Bad verbs give rise to adverbs,* she would say. *Choose the right verb.*
Samuel L. Johnson was equally verb-obsessed.

Waste and the environment. The unknowableness of being alive. The race to keep up. Just as you get used to a scenario, a person, a season, an age, a weight, a height, a schedule, a political situation – things change. Life is a racing current against the tides. We are always in opposition to our decaying selves, in opposition to being one of many, in opposition to having no control of anyone or anything, including oneself. We make our comforts and distractions, our systems, our routines and rituals.

Under The Sword? A white horse gallops across the field behind the dyke. *Der Kleine Pferd? Der Weisse Pferd?* Stefan Zweig? Got it: *Der Schimmelreiter*, Theodor Storm.

Akutagawa's 'The Story of a Head That Fell Off' begins with a head that knows that it is a head soon to fall off. *I'm cut, I'm cut,* he says, the voice, the consciousness that sits inside. As the head prepares to fall – at last, climax, chorus – the horse, with the head flopped over its mane, gallops across the field, the ghostly spectral presence that the rider on the white horse sees in the storm. One horse from one story jumps into another. A line is drawn. The man's head is cut. Under the line, his past – ten minutes earlier. In battle they sharpened each other's swords. We don't know this man, this warrior, in war. He was very successful.

The Making of Americans: repeating, then, is a way of repeating. Slowly, everyone comes to be clearer to someone. An ordered history of everyone. The Chinese warrior and the Japanese warrior sharpening each other's swords in the field. He was wailing, we are told, because of the dizzying ebb and flow of his emotions, centering on his fear of death. Go on existing. Family living can go on existing. They are quite certain. And anyone can come to be a dead one. A diatribe against war, and the nonsense of a man fighting a man in a field, sharpening their swords on each other, such that some can come to be dead ones. Family living. Some become dead ones. Not anyone then is remembering any such thing. Everyone is then a dead one. A diatribe against the nonsense of existing. *If I Told Him, A Completed Portrait of Picasso*. Would he like it? Xiao Er was overcome by a mysterious loneliness. Disappearing. Now all actively repeated. And do they do: A Modern Tragicomedy. Life is a modern tragicomedy. He, he, he, and he, as he, and he is, and as he is, he is and as he, and as he is, and he, and he. Oh, his head fell off, years later. He fell and hit the floor and his head fell off. A fairy tale. A modern fable. Let me recite what history teaches. And the story of the man lying in the ditch looking up at the sky, seeing mirages of home, is repeated. Retold.

A dream. Jumpers on a hill: young people, crouched like stones. I walk in a stone-walled trench. I need the toilet. *Ask the jumpers*, a girl says. I'll get them to write it on the rocks. To my left, people on a grassy bank say there's a toilet behind them. A cubicle houses a squat latrine. Dirty. Pubes. I don't go. I jump onto a two-tier display in a warehouse. I am with a man; he is looking for me.

Slipping around in the mud on the edges of the river. Feet depress sand: *schlunk, glunk*. Suction. Feet will not pull out. Panic. Hold still. Slowly pull. Leave the boots. Get to the edge. Escape the tide. The tide comes in fast. Sit now, momentarily peaceful, next to the hull of a houseboat. See how the water has pooled up behind you. You must wade now to regain the road. Heart races. Excitement. A thrill. Boots left behind. Walk barefoot along the riverside. Find a new pair of shoes: trainers slung up in a tree.

A dream. I am camping with people I don't know. I bought and then lost a coat. Now, in a shop, I find a second-hand version of the lost coat, as well as the coat I bought and lost. I try both on. It is agreed that the one I bought previously is best. We go into a field where we have each pitched a tent. A small girl lets a ball chase around a course she created. It's an artwork. This small girl is clearly Mystery from the film *Inside Out*. The girl is unhappy that I'm not more impressed by her artwork. I explain that I'm tired. The other five have put a large tent across all the small tents. I walk with some others back to my tent. It's gone. We find it pushed down a slope. We recover it and walk up to our larger encampment past a toilet tent in which four girls are using Shewees. They snarl at us. I'm with a girl with red hair in pig tails. We talk about community. *Surely it's better to embrace community, even when we're too many,* I say.

I know I'm in London when I see a stained old mattress propped against a wall. In the 1980s, when I lived in Brixton, there was always a mattress propped against a wall. To me it's a sign of tolerance and efficiency. A declaration from a society brave enough to show its face, warts and all, and offer up its detritus to whoever wants it. The waste ecology of the city. Slavoj Žižek in *Examined Life* says: *accept a person warts and all.*

> Cat climbing trellis,
> half-in and half-out, pauses –
> its arse towards me.

The mechanical beast idles as it gulps the clanking jars and bottles, the flattened cardboard boxes, the plastic cartons and lids, the clinking cans. I sit in the garden beneath the magnolia.

Meditation on a novel: a body of prose – waste prose – wasteful prose – waste-making prose – waste-making writing-making – lists as landscape – to what end – what takes place in that landscape? In *Life A User's Manual*, a man spends his life doing what he can to make his life meaningless. This involves lots of money and lots of people; lots of travel and activity; a whole lot of something.

Spatial relations between objects and meaning.

In Don de Lillo's *Underworld*, a character has waste in his car, which he is fly-tipping for a friend who runs a restaurant. This friend doesn't want to get into the car because the waste stinks. In 2015, in Southwark, waste doesn't stink because it's separated: food/recycling/general. Later, there's a garbage strike in New York.

On walking: "Bronzini thought that walking was an art. He was out nearly every day after school, letting the route produce a medley of sounds and forms and movements, letting the voices fall and the aromas deploy in ways that varied, but not too much, from day to day [...]. Bronzini didn't own a car, didn't drive a car, didn't want one, didn't need one, wouldn't take one if somebody gave it to him. Stop walking, he thought, and you die."[1]

If we knew how to live in houses we wouldn't make waste. Does anyone need a sofa, for instance? The only reason it seems important is psychologically: better to sit or lie on a sofa to watch a movie in the designated communal space of the living room than to do so in your bedroom, which feels squalid, even though it's still you, in a room, doing what you're doing. Why not go the whole hog and shove the sofa and TV out on the front lawn or yard or street? Let it all hang out.

1 DeLillo, D. (1998) *Underworld*, pp. 661-662.

RECYCLINGS

UNDERWORLD

bolts

sunblock tube

can of iced tea

clothes map rifle

muslin polymers cots

tents sleeping-bags badge

brush sandblaster T-shirts mike-boom

clipboard face-masks shirts jackets director's chair

cane bucket pants blazer photographs T-shirt blazer

necklace rings running-shoe sock elastic-brace cup clipboard

camera jeans tote-bag badge chair Nat-Sherman-blazer metal-primer cushion pants tools chair coffee-table books photograph

Turbo-blades rack postcards Indian-dolls

kachina-dolls sign TV house-keys ankle-wallet

house–keys ankle–wallet magazine dishwasher

TV TV television set humidifier dresser

dresser mirror hangers phone

hangers moon–suits

drums bottle

carton glass cans

paper glass glass tin

aluminium containers caps

lids newspapers twine phones

fax–machines photocopiers computer

pencil table computer rotating–media–shelves

bumper–sticker wireless–headphone ethnic–jewellery

bracelets chains photos books books ankle–wallet bill photograph photo bat dungarees TV hawser rope saddle dresser air–

conditioner mattress TV shorts cap

sneakers computer clothes wax-paper

cereal-boxes bins newspapers cans

jars cans bottles bins tin

aluminium paper-bag

paper-bags paper-bag

bags bag wax-paper

newspapers twine

TV apron coat

fedora

hawser

magazine paper

paper dishwasher TV

mirror bed birth-certificate

sign underwear bags bags toothpaste-tube

suit basket trunks T-shirt towel undershirt

singlet blade brush cup blade towel phone

tractor-parts catalogs boxes slacks carpeting paintings

jerseys socks condoms condoms latex-gloves books manuals videos T-shirts caps condoms rubbers condoms candy-jars finger-

condoms full-body-condoms oral-condoms

condom-cases condom hat cylinder condoms

Roman-coins condoms matchbook-folders

boxes condoms condoms condoms

condoms boxer-shorts glasses

spoons condoms box

sheath condom

computer

shipping-container

shipping-container

computer plastic-baggies

filter air-conditioner TV jeans

tank-top glass port-glass port-glass

port-glass pencil box glass sofa piano

piano bearskin books sofa wall-hanging

books TV books TV case mirror TV shorts cap computer videotape-device cigarettes radio radio cards bottles bins paper cereal-

boxes humidifier hangers bed dresser shirt telephones

washer packaging car-radio blade caps lids sticker

bumper-sticker apron coat hard-hat miner's-lamp

graveclothes basket tanks valves wires

instruments coiled rope nylon balloon

envelope balloon basket iron-bar

basket basket sweater bed

shelves carpets

magazine

page page

book-pillow

cushion book

magazine page

carpets page page

armchair baseball baseball

bookshelves books books books

baseball chair ball baseball ball ball

baseball ball bookshelves ball armchair

lamp slippers bed weapon baseball bookshelves

armchair baseball chair baseball armchair lamp palama-shirt bookshelves baseball radio   radio.

BLOW UP: TV, FRIDGE, CHICKEN

Middle right of frame, a square of white with a diagonal framework. Bottom, quarter in from left, the top of a red item. Midway, bottom of frame, a white shape with red protuberance. Further along to the right, beneath the kite-shaped item, cloud-like explosions, grey tipped with white.

CUT TO: quarter in, left, bottom of frame, an exploding item manifests cloudlike, its red protuberance ascends the frame at mid-point, bottom, and expands widthways. Right side of frame, cloudlike explosions, grey, tipped with white, expand widthways into a sectional shape: left side fuzzy white, middle section grey flecked and wispy, right side a creamy triangle shape, which folds inwards on making contact with the kite shape above.

CUT TO: quarter in, left, bottom of frame, the red protuberance tip, now a cone of grey and white smoke, out of which expands a wave of petrol grey crested with pale blue. Right of this and above, sticks, bones and knives concertina upwards. The white shape with red protuberance, haloed now with white cloudy powder, mid-point in the frame, is level with the grey cone to its left. To the right, the kite shape sprouts an underhang of chicken feet; behind this, a black bunny shadow. The red protuberance dissolves into a red powder puff, like the glorious red mist I imagine drifts into the atmosphere as Katharina Grosse transforms Fort Tilden's decaying aquatics building in the Rockaways into a colourful work of art. The red protuberance is now a heart; above which, a wig of white; above which, sticks, rulers, and a rack of some sort. Mid-frame, a quarter in from the left: a UFO, silver blue. Far right, mid-frame: the kite collides with a red anemone, which sits atop brown shoulders; beneath which, yellow chicken feet.

CUT TO: all the reds. The red protuberance, left of frame, is now one point of an otherwise white trapezoid. The red heart becomes a flop of innards, stuck barnacle-like to an orange hunk of something. Mid-point bottom of the frame a red stripe within a white rectangle. Sticks, squares, rectangles. The kite becomes a layer beneath which items explode downwards. Right, bottom of the frame: a white chair. Far left bottom: a puff of red. A third of the way in from the left, at the top of the frame, the kite has a tail of red, beneath which, a boulder of *papier-mâché*. Far right top, a curl of grey: a ram's antler. From below, cloudy white smoke explodes upwards into a blue sky, tinged with grey. A third of the way in from the right, the kite shape reveals itself as a parasol, attached to the skeleton of a white tubular garden table. A red ellipsis merges into the cream parasol above the circular frame of the table top.

CUT TO: two covered rails of clothes, assembled against the sky. The clothes implode, twisting as if on a centralised line of string, fire cloud behind, white smoke clouds and charred discs float up and out into the blue sky. ZOOM IN to the coloured rags as the rails collapse into the centre, coverings flinging up. Certain items – green, red, orange – now float upwards, like astronauts untethered.

CUT TO: view from above as heat sucks the clothing items upwards. Reds, mauves, orange, white, yellow, blue against a petrol grey smoky sky. Small shiny black-white flakes proliferate.

CUT TO: still life of a cathode ray TV, to its left a comfortable, upholstered chair; on top of the TV, a vase of yellow flowers pleasingly positioned towards the right edge, away from the chair. The anchorman's head and shoulders – short dark hair parted to the right, black rimmed glasses, white shirt, black jacket, black narrow tie – sits central on the screen. The fingers of his left hand, centre bottom, point out towards the viewer. The TV, which sits on a TV stand with chrome framework and teak veneer shelves, explodes in a rush of grey smoke. Its wooden sides fold up right and left to hold a fireball, which is overtaken rapidly by grey clouds of smoke filled with crystalline shards – grey, white and black, bubbles of white. A black speaker flies out to the right, hangs briefly mid-frame, then rotates out of frame to the right.

CUT TO: a smoke-filled frame. To the left: a brown-black bodily mass with yellow beaked head and two silver claws projecting down. Nests of black wiring and pieces of shiny metal tumble and turn. Spidery masses of black, silver threads.

CUT TO: still life of a tall fridge, its door open to reveal cartons, bottles and jars. It explodes as if from the bottom up. Flames rage left of frame as the fridge tips backwards.

CUT TO: colourful shapes fluttering against a blue sky like tossed confetti. Right, bottom of frame: a fish. As it rises, its slit inner opens like a gash. Beneath: a courgette. Entering right: a pink lobster. Far left: an egg.

CUT TO: white shapes and clouds explode outward. Mid-left, bottom, a packet of Special K ascends. Mid-screen, a circle of black. All items rise. Third of the way in, bottom right, a joint of meat ascends as the black disc disappears into the top of the frame. Below Special K, a carrot. A headless chicken enters the frame, bottom right. It rotates until bottom up and drifts out of frame to the far right. In the background, a mobile of red onion, orange, white onion, peach, red pepper.

CUT TO: a frieze of garments against a blue sky – red, white, pink, red and white striped, black, green. A pair of blue jeans far right.

CUT TO: metal pieces floating down.

CUT TO: books, pages, flecks of white.

CUT TO: neck ties close up, left of frame. Brown-patterned, colourful, striped, paisley green.

CUT TO: a Wonder loaf, upside-down, top left of frame. An apple beneath. Mid, bottom of frame, blurred: a bottle. Red blobs left, bottom, central and right; white flecks. The loaf, LARGE, exits, frame left.

CUT TO: a newspaper, floating in top right.

CUT TO: the garden table and parasol, white cloud of smoke left of frame and central, black smoke beneath the table, an item entering the frame third of way in from left, top of frame, looks like an upside-down doll.

CUT TO: a blue sky and items rising up from right side bottom of frame. A rising up. Books and papers. The screen fills with books as they spill and turn, vulnerable innards revealed.

CUT TO: rows of books suspended on a framework. The entire library articulates outwards; books open out like blooming roses as they fly towards the screen.

953

Red stands at the black cliff edge. There seeing gold flashes and silver explosions arising from the bow of a red sailing ship. They will all be showing their white teeth, lips blue, Red decides.

A long climb down. Scratchy sea thistles at ankle and calf. Salt-stunted chicory, blue petals narrow and straight like short ties. Yellow bobbles of broom. Red sky at night, shepherd's delight; but now it's morning, shepherd's warning. Half way down the cliff path, the moss-yellow and mould-black tin roof of help: the only man who can ride a dinghy across storm waves in sou'wester faded white.

Gate posts support a painted gate, closing off a picket fence.

Here, on this cliff edge.

Unruly containment.

She was a lifeguard once. White type across her tee-shirted tits. No one had required saving.

Teeth.

She sees them. Open mouths, exiting frothy vomit.

Know the red heart that beats inside; save it and not the white teeth.

Years Ago

Hat?
Or cap?
Which hat goes with this robe?
Which cap goes with that robe?
I will wear no undershirt.
Only a robe.
Naked beneath this robe.
All fur robe and no knickers.

Speedway

Statues wrapped in gold and silver foil, piles of firewood, corpses and droppings circle the brazier lit with coals.

Take your sword and slay the spiderwebs. These will cover the corpses; corpses like clay-dolls, the corpses, corpses.

Light a pine-stick.

This corpse, this body, lit by this pine-torch, resembles that corpse.

This corpse's hairs assemble: cut and laid out halo-like around the head, each hair separated from the other by a minuscule degree.

Each hair points in a different direction, lit by the pine-torch.

This hair, #2036, is longer than this hair, #1058.

This corpse, which lies adjacent to and touching the other, left hand to right hip, is no match for the sword that our man, a lowly servant, raises.

These corpses will know nothing now of his sword.

The old woman speaks: "You will cut their hair; we will make a wig."

Our lowly servant considers these hairs of this corpse, strand-like, not web-like.

"This is dead hair. Just as dead snakes may be dried fish," she says.

This is now life and death.

Raise your sword.

Corpses.

He gazes upon the body: hers, and the corpses.

[A] Western

Cricket
Cricket
Fleas

953 [2]

Rain
Rain
[Earthquakes]
[Whirlwinds]
Rain
Rain
Rain
Rain
Rain
Rain
Chill
Wind
Wind
Rain
Rainy it is.

Speedway [2]

Foxes eat badgers which eat crows which prefer to not eat crows that eat crows; a dog, a lizard and a monkey confront the chicken, the predator-bird's crow, offering it snakes instead of fish: 'fish'.

Reggae

On eating sesame seeds I am apt to sneeze.
On eating dried fish I forget to breathe.
Not when eating fish.

She sat, waiting, and was clinging to the edge of her seat, which was situated – could have been/was – in the hull of a boat. She was conscious of, and had been struck by, the idea to join life, leading to actions by which, she tells us, she would smash through all that had gone before, pile all past convictions clinging, and sell.

Bothered, she and I came to live.

We were joined, and abandoned things we made.

She avoided the eyes of birds, which flocked overhead, and would unsettle, cawing, circling. I turned. She stood. The bird, a crow, came to peck. We were silent, not wanting to be seen. Nearby in the hull was a dead seal carcass that sprouted monstrous crops of fungal plume. We had settled, worrying. A mist had formed; not fixed, but noted, as if it was waiting, as we had. What was I going to do? If something else had happened, would I have returned? I had been dismissed. She, I noted, was stoic. She had served the same dream as me; she was alone, she was waiting. It would have been like this whatever. I had to go, to do as others; contribute. Back then snow had been falling. Nothing showed. I went on, poured myself along. I was determined to find out a truth, to keep the faith, to do what was expected to be done. I carried the burdens that came to envelop me, and brought me to this. I was supporting her, and everyone, to do what had to be done, what would have to be done, but I hesitated. All that would be carried was discarded. It was as if I wandered in a fog. I passed through states of being that remained cold. I was told I was prepared to do it, could find my strength. They had given me a truncheon, and dragged me to the beach, where I was to make a catch. A baby seal, isolated. I yearned for something, a long-dead nostalgia, even as the truncheon fell. I blew its brains out and it was gone. I hunched down, drew short breaths, scanned the beach. Were we alone? Could my action have viewers? Would they stay?

I caught sight of her now leading a dog. *She is taking care not to slip along rocks set into the sand to avoid erosion.* She crouched, holding her dog. I took stock, cast around, my innards inflamed. I hadn't considered this scenario. It could be, I realised, not moving – as I saw her dog's tail flickering, as the sea mist hung – it could be… as a burning sensation crept from head to toes, hunching me as she stretched and peered… that she saw, and had said to herself, that to tell was wrong. She had thought this would be it, and now she can see what we are, who we are, where we are. *She is tangled: in her hair, in the fur of the dog, in the rush of sea spray.* It was in order for me to believe in what had been that I looked. Who was lying?

She flung her arm out. I caught sight of her casting her notions. She reached me and I flew to her. *She's forgot, memory obliterated, until she catches sight of me crouching in front of her.*

Dressed still in the yellow gown, I was in front of her, and still held the truncheon. She stared. *Judging by that look, small eyes in beaten face, she is moved, forgetting to breathe. As if to borrow my breath, I feel her eyes are growing.*

Hands placed on my chest, my heart, my lungs. She examined me, searching, began plucking at my skin, and then seemed to slip. *Her beastliness gives way, disappears, replaced by what can be misleading. A noise is felt, grows.* What were we there to present? What had been the idea overall? To starve to death? To turn to butchery? Would I have been chosen if I had blazed up, had stood against them? I had. She was pulling. I could not call. She, plucking, was suddenly something I recalled. This is what we had been planning. I leaped up, still grasping the truncheon. I strode towards her, crouched, leaped, launched the truncheon into the air, shouted, blocked her path. She stumbled to flee, struggled to break. She pushed. I grappled. She was cold. I grasped her hand, twisted her arm, demanded things, shoving, as the sea swept by. I thrust the dog ahead of us. 'Now,' I said, trembling, heaving, straining. She kept still, she struggled. *She is seeing something else,* I realised.

Governed by hate, hope cooled. It had been burning. I felt it, looked it, spoke it. She happened to be passing, I won't lie. She tied up the dog, not taking it away.

I want to tell her what I've been doing. The dog stretched. She stared. It had something in its mouth, chewing. I moved. *It seems she cannot see me move.* Until she issued a protest. I reached the seal.

Above, a crow was cawing, and pulling, pulling at the innards of the now-butchered seal. The dog startled. She, disappointed that I turned out to be like this. She came across to fill her lungs with the rancid air. *She senses what I feel, still holding the truncheon I stole.* I mumbled, croaked, offered to be wrong, to pull the seal out of the birds' reach.

I deserve what I get.

She took the truncheon from me. I was already pulling the seal. "That woman used to cut, dry, and sell seal meat," I said. "If she hadn't died, she'd still be selling it. People loved it; they bought it every day. I don't think I was wrong to do what I did, to keep from starving to death. I couldn't help it. Don't think what I'm doing is any different to what everyone is doing; it's logical, we can't help it. If I don't do it, what do I have to do?"

I think she understands. She is doing something, slowly.

Her hand returns to her side, truncheon down. She is resting. She has listened. We have played. I have listened.

An idea began to germinate.

What I lacked was knowledge that something was moving. I felt impelled at that moment to seize a beast, an animal that was there. I felt torn, I was starving to death. *But in becoming like everyone else I'm now banished from society, from myself. I have become that which I would have pressed anyone not to become.*

Stepping forward now I shot out my arm, grasped her by the throat. She bit me. I won't blame her for that, for taking that opportunity. We all have to do whatever to keep from starving to death. I stripped her of the dark coat. She tried to clutch it. I gave her a push that sent her sprawling, and brought her coat to my shoulders, tucking it around me.

She plunged.

I did this last thing, which was to take the seal that had been lying beneath me, raised it up, muttering, groaning, crawled to the boat's edge, hung the seal overboard, peered into the sea and saw nothing.

What happened next, who knows?

[The] Western

This evening, the calamity of the preceding years, in which I and all I know have found themselves in decline, we experience emotional turmoil. X proposes a new custom. This is necessary to allay the rumours that talk of the great emotion manifesting as a smell: of terror, curiosity, fear, loathing; loathing and revulsion.

"The notion of evil must be debated," states X. "We will do so daily at 6pm. We will suffuse emotion and find strength. For each minute that we face the choice between starvation and regret, our hatred can only breed evil. This idea compels us towards enacting a deed that may be good, but most likely will be evil, and this evil must not be lost sight of. If we silence it, there will be struggle. Have no doubt that in silence there is no life, only death. With our will and awareness, we can banish hatred, rediscover pride. In this we will feel satisfaction. This is now our new job. To banish the hatred and contempt in our collective heart."

With this explanation, X appears to slay death. Death is no longer the story. Courage, courage, courage is the song which will defer death. In our collective mind we consider death and our consciousness of it with mockery. To death we say night, night.

EMOTIONAL PAYLOAD

CLAP, CLAP, CLAP, CLAP, CLAP, ———, ———, —,
COUGH, COUGH ———, **urgh,** ——— cough, cough, — —
cough, ——, **de rrr k, d,** cough, —————, —, cough, ——, cough,
——, cough, ————, cough, ———, —, cough, ——, cough, —,
cough, —— , cough, cough, ———, ———, cough, cough, cough,
cough, cough, —, SHOUT, *paper sounds*, cough, **umpa, vrwrrrr,**
rrrrr, aaaaaaa, n st, ck, k, fsut, cough, **ahh,** *mouth noise,* **re er eeeres,**
uuuu, ll ll, grr grj rrr, r fffff, cough, cough, chatter, **chit, chit ep bo**
sleeps, what, freeees, p, cough, cough, *paper rustle......, mouth noise,*
cough, cough, **thy, rrrrrrr, think, threeeee, rinding, to the thee, of**
the shar do, if is, and hard, kering dis, mmmmm, to, ar k his gld,
in dee, cough, *rustle*, **should, ing, and, unsealed soul**. Cough. Titter.
Applause. Cough. Chitter chatter. C̲l̲a̲p̲. C̲l̲a̲p̲. **Put. Rrrbo.** C̲l̲a̲p̲.
C̲l̲a̲p̲. Chitter. Whistle. Laugh. **Chin wook**. Applause. **And these**.
'Yeay.' Whistle. **And whess rrr.** C̲l̲a̲p̲. **To go**. Applause. **Hnnrrr.**
Gnhh. Applause. Whistle. **Eeee. Eee**. Chatter. **To heel. Arc p.**
C̲l̲a̲p̲. C̲l̲a̲p̲. Shout. Cough. 'Keep it up John.' Laugh. Whoop. Ho ho.
Ung s strong. Bravo. Applause. Laugh. Chatter. **Fff. Eeeeeeeeeeee**.
Applause. **Flo. Ing nt har**. 'America.' **Oo. Bul**. Whistle. **Set. Grr.**
Ee. Whistle. **Ent. Rlll**. Whistle. **Well. One**. Cough. **See**. Chat. **Ish**
we fry p plu. Most. Of. Ebor brrrrannnn. Applause. **Oh. Un stir de**
bok ro. I now sting. Ey or. Ee. Chris. Sss. Days. Sss. *Mouth noise.*
Lick lips. **Eeear. Oh. Sat. Ulcrnn. Avblue. Astrgtga vishower. Let**
in losre. Forsart. Tck a tcuk. Laugh. Cough. Cough. *Mouth noise.*
Cough. Pause. Pause. Chat. Pause. Applause. **To. Ree. Glin. Urrrr**.
Cough. **Woohhae. Lnd to wrrrrrrrrrrrrrrrrrrrrrrrr**. Laugh. 'Oh.'
E ear to ft. Russrrr. Shout. **Eeee. Oohhh. Oh tos stirn rrrrrrr**.
Mouth noise. **Rrrrrrrrrrrrrrrrrrrrrgh**. Chat. Whistle. C̲l̲a̲p̲. Whistle.

Whop. Se be. Urrrll. Urll. Pall. Appallll. Oh. *Rustle*. 'Buon giorno.'
Oh dee. Slunk sl. Id. Um. Unt glue to brgh. Hrgh. Um. Ulll.
'Allora!' Whistle. Applause. **Uhhh**. <u>Clap</u>. <u>Clap</u>. **Ho hle cr underm
ma hooo**. Shout. Whistle. Shout. **Sat oh. Hwisly. Ee warld**. Chat.
Grunt. Shout. Whistle. **Snoww**. Chatter. **No days**. Whistle. Chatter.
Applause. Chanting. **From and large. Them much chr**. Whistle.
Chatter. Whistle. Chatter, _, _, _. Chatter. *Mouth noise*. 'John.' *Mouth
noise*. **A long ee ds d by song ven**. Whistling, shouting, banging,
drumming. 'We are not Italian.' Noisy shouting, clapping, drumming,
banging, shouting. **Sssssssssss**. Banging, drumming, banging,
drumming, banging, drumming, faster, louder. **Aaaan, noo, ssssssssk,
ssss**. Banging, drumming, shouting, WHISTLE, shout. **Chhhuuuu**.
BANG. **Feee**. WHISTLE. **Un dis mayyy chaan**. Drumming,
whistling, bang bang bang, drumming, shouting, whistling, shouting,
whistling. **Now cld. OWWWWWW**. BANG. **Wwaa tha**. <u>CLAP</u>.
Man. Chant, <u>CLAP</u>, shout. **Paro**. <u>Clap</u>. **And ap, no way**. <u>CLAP</u>.
Bang. **Rrrrrrrrrrrr, wiythuuuuuuuuuuuuuuuuuuum**. Shouting,
banging, shouting, slow claps. FEET STAMP. **Wwwoooow**. WAR-
CRIES CLAPPING CHANTING FEET-STAMPING IN
STRONG STEADY RHYTHM, whistling. **Ssssss, ttttt, ullllll,
wwoooooo, woop**. WAR CRIES. **Ooolll laa laaa _ ooo ca un ung _**
whistle shout stamp <u>Clap</u> WHISTLING WHISTLING chanting
<u>clapping</u> Rhythmic stamping. **Soousooo, ouch, oooi, and run**.
Shouting, shouting. **Win my, ung**. 'WOO! WOO!' Chat chat chat
SHOUT. **ArrrrrrrrrrrrrrrrrrrrrrrrrrrrrrrrrRRRRRRRrrrrrrrrrrrrrrrr**.
RHYTHMIC STAMPING and <u>CLAPPING</u> and WHISTLING,
shouting. **Lasssielbosessbeeeee**. WAVES OF SHOUTING
WHISTLING CHATTING SHOUTING <u>CLAPPING</u>
WHISTLING RHYTHMIC BEATING BANG. **Rrrrrrr**.
SHOUT. **Adrwkwithdr, rees, post scrr de war**. SHOUTING,
WHISTLING, <u>CLAPPING</u>, SHOUTING, RHYTHMIC
BEATING FASTER FASTER 'EY! EY! EY!' **Ap train pft pfff**

ch wwOWOW yoiiii. WHISTLING WHISTLE WHISTLE arlllLLLLLLLLLllll _ eeeee _. CHATTING CLAPPING SINGING WHISTLING _ shouting _ chatting. llldes, nnng. Shouting. Ng guuuu. Shouting. Harrrrrrsts, east t re yoAL say go lrrr. RHYTHMIC BEATING CLAPPING STAMPING _ shouting _ frenzied stamping 'OFF! OFF! OFF! OFF! rhythmic frenzied rattling of what, spoons? A mmmmmmmmmrrr CRRRR. 'WOO!' Marn na gsss sl. Shouting WHISTLING WHISTLING shouting. Paaa sysscla doooo, turnnnns sae. Shouting chatting CLAP CLAP CLAP CLAP CLAP SCREAM BANG SCREAM. Me hup. SHOUT SHOUT SHOUT. Expemens string naaaa ss. CHATTER. Ahhh vsssss lois. SHOUTING SHOUTING SHOUTING SHOUTING SHOUTING SHOUTING SHOUTING SHOUTING SHOUTING SHOUTING _ whistle _ CHATTER. Vildin ee vistens so do. WHISTLE, clap, clap, chatter, chatter, shout, chatter. Oohhhhh llllLLLLLLLLLLLLLllllll risoooo arrrrrrssssssslllllLLlll viskll OHL. SHOUTING. Rrr rrr ssppp spp tee vl brr rrrrr rrrrrr spppppp. CHAT CHAT CHAT CHAT CHAT CHAT. Sdon s eel arrlll a non. SHOUTING. Sena de neta un rli vooo rrrrrrrhhhrrrl arrrrrr rrrrvoo. SHOUTING chatter. Vo ve fe ha. SHOUTING 'WOO!' CHATTER chatter SHOUTING, shouting. Arm st to dii som. CLINK CHANT CHANT CHANT chatter SHOUT. Nerfee er chhr ree stus. CLAP CLAP CLAP. Ar ma di. WHOOP CHEER CHANT WHOOP. Whoooo whooohoooowhoooowhoooowhoooowhhooo _ do ma say. 'CUCKOO! CUCKOO.' Whooooohoooowhooohhhohwwhohwhhoo _ rl, mach ar bee bar _ whooohoooohoooowhooohoooowhoooohwhohohooo. WHISTLE. Whhohohhoooohohooooowhhooowhooo. 'CUCKOO! CUCKooo!' Mne et a no. Whohoohwhhoohhoooo. CLAP CLAP CLAP CLAP CLAP. FlluuughhHHhhhh rsayo tk de st reai yor. SHOUT. Dsppr dsipr liso. CLAP CLAP CHAT

42

SHOUT <u>CLAP</u>. **Ssss drrrr rrrrr rr ssssoo rleEEEEEEEEEEeee** **ughhhh _ AHHHHHHHHHH _ u rrrr.** SHOUT _ chatter. **Tng e rrrrllllllllll trrrrrrrr _ fkk rrrrrrr ulll librrrarrrrrr.** SHOUTING. **Rrrrrr.** DESPERATE SCREAMS _ CHATTER SHOUTING. **Kssssssr rrrryes.** SHOUTING _ SHOUTING _ CHANTING _ SHOUTING _ bang _ SHOUTING _ bang. **ssssssspprrrwwwwaaaaaa** <u>CLAPPING</u> **slapaismfr mcinar** SHOUTING <u>CLAPPING</u> _ SHOUTING. **Arrr on ris stuuu rrrn.** SHOUTING 'BRAVO! BRAVO!' <u>CLAP</u> <u>CLAP</u> <u>CLAP</u>. **Oh ar.** SHOUT SHOUT shouting. **Oh rrarrrrr _ shee rrrrr snnnni.** SHOUTING _ 'Compagnie!' **Ah gi, sky rrrrrrr.** SHOUTING. **It pee rrrrRRRRRRrrrra, sp ear iuuuu.** CHAT CHAT SHOUTING CHAT CHAT. **Sssssssssppppppppp.** SHOUTING. **Rrrr.** Mimicking: 'RRRR AHHH RRRR!' **Rrrddrr.** 'I love you.' Tarzan hollas. **Sssss rdd dddddrrrr ss.** CHAT CHAT CHAT. **Oor rr.** SINGING SINGING. **Tu brn a ov r sx dir wer sn.** CHAT. **Urn d las so.** SHOUT <u>CLAP</u> SHOUT. **Ungggggggnnn.** 'John Cage e sumero. John Cage.' SCREAMS SCREAMING WHISTLING _ <u>CLAPPING</u>. **Lllll shhh pshrw ssshh.** 'Compagnie!' 'Response.' **Hnn swww diiiii ssssw va lllee rwrrwrwrwrr wassa.** 'You are stupid, you are stupid, you are very stupid. Compagnie, John Cage o non?' **Hiym hon.** SHOUTING SHOUTING SHOUTING. **Rest lu rya some have white ones dddddddddrrrr vvrrrrrr, of two srt was das srm arm lon foot.** <u>CLAPPING</u> <u>CLAPPING</u> _ SHOUTING SHOUTING SHOUTING SHOUTING CHATTING CHATTING. **Thee r myrrr r us rrrrrrr.** SHOUTING. **Is it's s ban these bv vsss reee in a in ooo and a.** SHOUTING. **Hv ri kr thee.** SHOUTING SHOUTING CHANTING CHANTING CHANTING CHANTING. **Rrrrrrr eeeee ooo furrrar ooooo sssssssss oooooooo rrrrrrrrr.** SHOUT. **Rrrrr.** SHOUTING. 'Italian.' WHISTLING CHEERING 'Italian.' **Uurrr sssssss arr ooo sssscddd eeeee.** CHATTING.

At the end: rapturous applause.

Acknowledgements

bmbmbm is previously published, differently titled as *Rashomon: recycledverbstory,* by *Sublunary Editions*, Oct 2020.

Notes on the text

The text for UNDERWORLD is extracted from Don de Lillo's novel *Underworld* (1997): Part 1: Long Tall Sally: spring-summer 1992. BLOW UP: TV, FRIDGE, CHICKEN is a transcription of the blow-up scene in Michelangelo Antonioni's film *Zabriskie Point* (1969). The stories in RASHOMON RECYCLED are made by extracting component items of the story *Rashomon* (1915) by Ryūnosuke Akutagawa as follows: colours, clothing, objects, insects, weather, animals, food, verbs, abstract nouns, and using these lists of words to create new pieces. The titles are song titles from the album *Schlagenheim* (2019) by Black Midi. EMOTIONAL PAYLOAD transcribes a section of Cage's performance of *Empty Words* at Teatro Lirico, Milan, 1997.

The work in this pamphlet is extracted from a novel-in-progress/ hybrid text supported by an Arts Council DYCP grant.

Supported using public funding by

ARTS COUNCIL ENGLAND

LAY OUT YOUR UNREST
LAY OUT YOUR UNREST
LAY OUT YOUR UNREST
LAY OUT YOUR UNREST
LAY OUT YOUR UNREST
LAY OUT YOUR UNREST
LAY OUT YOUR UNREST
LAY OUT YOUR UNREST
LAY OUT YOUR UNREST
LAY OUT YOUR UNREST
LAY OUT YOUR UNREST
LAY OUT YOUR UNREST
LAY OUT YOUR UNREST
LAY OUT YOUR UNREST
LAY OUT YOUR UNREST
LAY OUT YOUR UNREST
LAY OUT YOUR UNREST
LAY OUT YOUR UNREST

www.ingramcontent.com/pod-product-compliance
Lightning Source LLC
Chambersburg PA
CBHW032113170626
46808CB00008B/3043